The Sleeping Beauty

The Sleeping Beauty

From The Brothers Grimm

retold and illustrated by
Trina Schart Hyman

LITTLE, BROWN AND COMPANY
Boston   Toronto

T 10-77

Library of Congress Cataloging in Publication Data

Hyman, Trina Schart.
  The sleeping beauty.

  SUMMARY: Enraged at not being invited to the princess'
christening, the thirteenth fairy casts a spell that
dooms the princess to sleep for one hundred years.
  [1. Folklore—Germany. 2. Fairy tales] I. Grimm,
Jakob Ludwig Karl, 1785–1863. Schneewitchen. II. Title.
PZ8.H994Sl   398.2'l   75-43769
ISBN 0-316-38702-9

*Published simultaneously in Canada
by Little, Brown & Company (Canada) Limited*

PRINTED IN THE UNITED STATES OF AMERICA

To the memory of Annie Wagner

A LONG TIME AGO there lived a King and a Queen who had no children, and this grieved them more than can be imagined. Every day they wished, "If only we had a child," but the days passed and they remained childless.

However, one day as the Queen was bathing in a forest pool, a little green frog came out of the water and said to her, "Your dearest wish shall soon be fulfilled. Before a year has passed you shall bring a daughter into the world." The Queen went home and told her husband what had happened, and sure enough, the frog's words came true.

The Queen gave birth to a little girl who was so very beautiful that the King could not contain himself for joy, and so he prepared a great feast. He invited all his friends, relatives, and noble acquaintances, and also the fairy women, so that they might be kindly disposed towards the child. Unfortunately, there were thirteen of these fairies in the kingdom, and the King owned only twelve golden plates. He was ashamed and afraid to ask one of them to dine from a silver plate. Therefore the oldest and most difficult of the fairies was not invited, and the King was secretly glad of an excuse to exclude her from the company.

The birthday feast was held with great splendor and merriment, and when it finally came to an end, each fairy presented the new baby with a magic gift. One gave her virtue, another grace, a third wisdom, and so on—everything in the world that the child could possibly wish for.

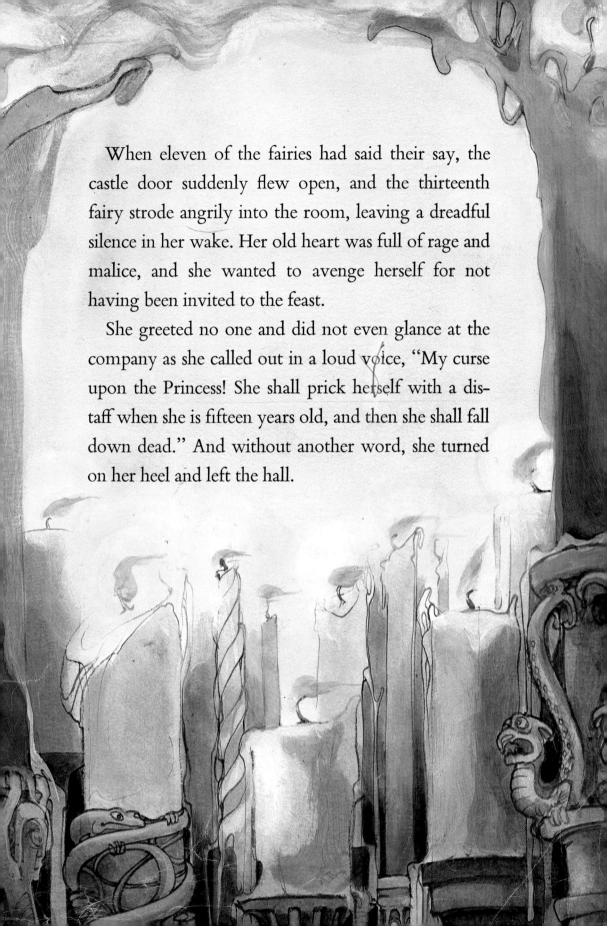

When eleven of the fairies had said their say, the castle door suddenly flew open, and the thirteenth fairy strode angrily into the room, leaving a dreadful silence in her wake. Her old heart was full of rage and malice, and she wanted to avenge herself for not having been invited to the feast.

She greeted no one and did not even glance at the company as she called out in a loud voice, "My curse upon the Princess! She shall prick herself with a distaff when she is fifteen years old, and then she shall fall down dead." And without another word, she turned on her heel and left the hall.

Everyone at the feast was terror-stricken and full of remorse, but the twelfth and youngest fairy, who had not yet given her wish, stepped forward. "Because of your discourtesy to a fairy woman," she said to the King, "I cannot change the curse but I can soften it a bit. So your daughter will not die, but instead she shall fall into a deep sleep which will last for a hundred years."

The poor King became sick with grief and worry. To guard his dear child from this misfortune, he sent out a command at once that all of the spinning wheels in the kingdom should be brought to the castle, and there they were burnt in a great fire. Anyone in the kingdom who kept a distaff faced the pain of death. After seven years had passed the King gradually forgot about the dreadful curse, and was finally content.

As time went on, all the wishes of the fairies came true. The Princess grew up so gracious, merry, beautiful, and kind that everyone who knew her could not help but love her. And because she was mischievous and clever as well, she was called Briar Rose.

Now it happened that on the very day when Briar Rose was fifteen years old, the King and Queen had to be away from home, and the Princess was left alone for the day to amuse herself. So she wandered about, all over the whole castle, looking at forgotten rooms and dusty halls, just as she pleased.

At last she came to a strange old tower that she had never seen before. She climbed the narrow staircase, until she became quite dizzy, and finally reached a little wooden door. A rusty key was stuck in the lock, and when she tried to turn it, the door opened swiftly and silently.

In the tiny room sat a toothless old woman, who was busily spinning a pile of flax on an ancient spinning wheel.

"Good day, Granny," said the Princess politely, "What are you doing?"

"I am spinning," said the old woman. "Come in, my child," and she smiled and nodded her head. The flax threw dusty golden motes into the air, and a silver thread seemed to grow from the distaff.

"Oh, what is that thing that whirls around so merrily?" asked the Princess. "How nice it looks! May I try it, please?"

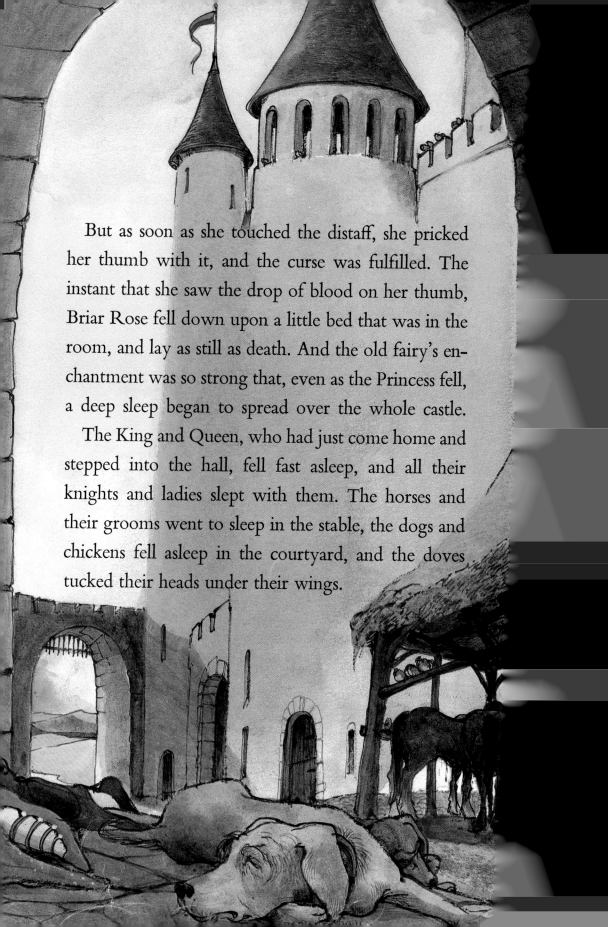

But as soon as she touched the distaff, she pricked her thumb with it, and the curse was fulfilled. The instant that she saw the drop of blood on her thumb, Briar Rose fell down upon a little bed that was in the room, and lay as still as death. And the old fairy's enchantment was so strong that, even as the Princess fell, a deep sleep began to spread over the whole castle.

The King and Queen, who had just come home and stepped into the hall, fell fast asleep, and all their knights and ladies slept with them. The horses and their grooms went to sleep in the stable, the dogs and chickens fell asleep in the courtyard, and the doves tucked their heads under their wings.

The flies on the wall stopped crawling; the fire on the hearth died down to a whisper, and even the roast meat stopped crackling. The cook, who was pulling the scullion's hair because he had made some mistake, let him go and went to sleep, and the kitchen maid dropped the hen she had been plucking and laid her head upon her arm. The wind dropped, and not a leaf stirred on the trees. All was silent and still as death.

The sky gathered up the seasons, and time went on. Gradually over the years, a hedge of thorny briar-roses grew round about the King's castle. Every year it grew higher, and the brambles and weeds grew stronger and thicker, until at last a great forest of stems and thorns surrounded the entire place. Nothing could be seen of it except a few ragged threads of the flags hanging from the roof.

But a legend grew up in the land about the lovely Princess who lay sleeping somewhere in an enchanted castle. From time to time brave young men came and tried to force a way through the briar hedge, but they could never find the Princess. They came with valiant dreams and hearts full of fire, but the thorns, like angry hands, held them fast and the young men remained caught in them and could not free themselves, and so they died a terrible death.

After many, many years a King's son came riding from a neighboring country. One summer evening, he stopped by the side of the road and shared his supper with an old man, who told him the story of the castle which stood behind the briar hedge. He heard all about the beautiful maiden who had been asleep for a hundred years, and also about the forgotten King and Queen, and of all their sleeping courtiers. The Prince remembered the old story from his childhood tales and he also remembered how, over the years, many brave men had come and fought to pierce through the terrible thorns, and had died a long, lonely death. He remembered how the Princess Briar Rose had come to him in his dreams and held out her hand. It was a childhood tale and a youthful dream, so the young Prince smiled and said, "Old man, I am not afraid. I would be happy to die for a chance to look upon the sleeping beauty."

The old man said everything he could think of to discourage him, but the Prince only laughed at all the gloomy words, and finally he rode away towards the castle.

And now, the hundred years were at an end. The day had come when Briar Rose was to wake up again. When the King's son approached the thorny hedge it was covered with hundreds of beautiful flowers. They made way for him of their own accord and let him pass unharmed, but then closed up again into a thorny hedge behind him.

As he rode into the courtyard he saw the hounds lying fast asleep, and in the stable nearby he saw the horses and their grooms, all sleeping. On the rooftops sat the doves with their heads tucked under their wings, and the flies were clustered like a crust all over the walls.

There was a terrible silence everywhere, and when he went into the castle, he needed all his courage to go on, for the musty smell of sleep was over everything. In the great hall, near their thrones, lay the King and Queen, with their knights and ladies sleeping all about them, as still as death. In the kitchen, there was the snoring cook and the scullion sprawled at his feet and the kitchen maid with her head on the table, a dead black fowl in her lap.

He went on farther, passing through forgotten rooms and dusty halls. His footsteps echoed through the silence, and it was all so still that he could hear his own heart beating.

At last he came to a ruined tower, and he climbed the narrow staircase and pushed open the door to the little room where Briar Rose was sleeping.

There she lay, amidst the dust and the cobwebs, looking so shining and beautiful and merry that he could not believe what he saw. His heart was so full of love that he knelt down beside her and gave her a kiss.

As soon as he touched her, the spell was broken; Briar Rose opened her eyes and looked wonderingly at him.

After a little while, they went down from the tower together, hand in hand. Where one drop of blood drains a castle of life, so one kiss can bring it alive again. Then the King and Queen woke up, and so did all their knights and ladies, and everyone looked at each other with astonishment in their sleepy eyes. The horses in the stable stood up and shook themselves, and the grooms scratched their heads and stretched their legs. The hounds began to leap about, barking at nothing and wagging their tails.

The rooster called a belated and mighty crow to his hens, and the doves on the roof lifted their heads from under their wings, looked surprised, and flew off into the fields. The flies on the wall began to crawl again, and the fire crackled up to roast the meat. The cook blinked his eyes and then boxed the scullion's ears so soundly that the poor boy cursed and howled. The kitchen maid went back to plucking the black fowl, and even the very stones of the palace slowly began to breathe again.

After a few days the wedding of the Prince and Briar Rose was celebrated with great feasting and splendor, and as they had waited so long for their happiness, you may be sure that they lived in peace and joy until they died.